Beloved of the Stars

PARENTAL ADVISORY: ADULT CONTENT
[This book does contain small amounts
of adult content. Parental discretion is
advised.]

Beloved of The Stars
written by Joseph "Prince Imoudu" Okoli

This book is the RAW unedited work of Joseph "Prince Imoudu" Okoli.

This work has been left in its original form and left unedited in order to keep the original energy and feel of the story.

All character names, events, and settings within this book are works of the author's imagination. Any similarities to actual people, names, places or events are purely coincidental.

Beloved of the Stars

[Scene 1]
Title: Boy Meets Girl
Location: Club X
Length: 5 minutes

DALLAS, TEXAS
UPTOWN

The scene begins outside of Club X. Music begins to play. We see the silhouettes of beautiful women wearing body contour dresses. The camera focuses on their legs, on back, and butt, but we do not focus on the looks of these women; they are not main characters. We see many cars in the parking lot. We hear the sound of engines; the night is here.

Veratis arrives, and is dropped off by a brown luxurious SUV with tinted windows. He steps out calmly. We first see his feet. He is looking crisp. He is wearing a clean pair of tree bark brown oxford shoes with slight broguing on the cap toe, tailored dress pants, and a crispy brand new medium red-white-and-blue polo shirt. Veratis stands confidently at about six feet tall, and the camera follows him as he walks through the club and up a flight of stairs, calmly, toward his unknown destination.

Music plays—adding to the feeling of the scene. As the camera follows Veratis, we see the sexy atmosphere of the club—drinks being poured, people conversing; it is a happening place.

On the second floor, two men from New Jersey are getting into an argument with each other. Two very large muscle bound bouncers are standing in between the men. Each of the bouncers are wearing black clean polos, and each of the men arguing are wearing white t-shirts. As heated words are thrown between the two men, (with the bouncers holding them back) Veratis manages to sneak right between the two bouncers, untouched, as the argument continues to escalate.

Veratis continues up yet another flight of stairs, and—
after almost one minute of the camera following him,
he reaches the bar on the third floor, and stands cooly
with his back to the bar, waiting for the bartender. His
hand is positioned in a certain type of way, with an
amount of cash in his hand, to draw the bartender's
attention. But he is not looking at the bar or the
bartender. He is focused on the inhabitants of the
nightclub. He is enjoying the atmosphere— seeing the
people, all of them, seeming to have fun.

The bartender summons Veratis's attention, and he
turns toward her. *He is stunned by her beauty.* She is
smoking hot. She is a beautiful bombshell.

Bartender is dressed in a classy spaghetti strapped
sundress, with her belt hugging her right below her
breasts.

Bartender speaks: Can I get you something.
[Veratis looks up]
Veratis speaks: Yes of course…
[Veratis pauses]
Veratis speaks: tú hablas español?
Bartender speaks: Sí… yes
Veratis speaks: Tú tienes novio?
Bartender speaks: No, no novio, no boyfriend.
Veratis speaks: Por qué No?
Bartender speaks: um… I don't know, I guess, no
qualified candidates.
Veratis speaks: Okay… well, that is nice… can I have
a shot of blue agave tequilla and a glass of ice water?
And if you'd like a drink for yourself, you can pour
yourself whatever you like.

[The music lowers, and we hear the thoughts of Bartender narrating. We see her conversing with Veratis as she begins to pour the drinks]

Bartender's thoughts: "there was a time when my mind was young, and my body was like a virgin's. I was a sophomore in college. I had never been with a boy. And I was not about to let any boy get in the way of me reaching the top."
[The scene ends]

[Scene 2]
Title: Semi-Secluded Stall inside of Club X
Location: Semi-Secluded Stall inside of Club X
Length: 5 minutes

[Veratis has Bartender consensually cornered in the bar. It is possible for people to see them, but they are in a somewhat secluded booth-stall, where people go to make out.]

Veratis speaks: You are so fuckin sexy.
[Bartender kisses and then bites Veratis's neck. Veratis begins to gently rub Bartender's [censored], through her panties. Veratis pulls down Bartender's top and begins to suck her small supple breasts. As Veratis sucks them, Bartender moans.]
Bartender speaks: That feels so good.
[Veratis begins to move her panties to the side. This is not shown on camera, but from her reaction we sense what is going on]

Bartender speaks: No no no, not here, not here
Veratis speaks: okay
[Bartender moves in and kisses Veratis on his lips.]
[Bartender takes a deep breath. . .]
Bartender speaks: That was hot!…..
Veratis speaks: We should get out of here.
Bartender speaks: I can't. I am at work. You should come with me to my place, after we close.

[Scene changes within the scene]
[We no longer see Veratis or Bartender, but for a few brief moments— for about 10 seconds— we see the inside of the club. We hear the music is still playing. We see people enjoying themselves. We see that the night is still young.]
[The scene ends]

[Scene 3]
Title: Bartender's Apartment
Location: Bartender's Apartment
Length: 5 minutes

[Bartender leads Veratis, holding his hand, as they approach her apartment door.]

Bartender speaks: Welcome to mi apartamento! [Bartender unlocks her door, and they enter. The apartment is very clean and modern.]

Bartender speaks: You can set your backpack in my room. Make yourself at home… I'm gonna use the bathroom.

[Veratis enters Bartender's kitchen and looks inside of her fridge. The fridge is well stocked with an assortment of food and drinks.]

Veratis enters Bartender's bedroom, sets his backpack down, and sits on her bed, testing out the bounce of the mattress. As he sits on the bed, he faces her closet and realizes that Bartender's sliding closet door is a gigantic mirror—perfect for taking pictures.

Veratis takes out his phone, and opens up his camera app.

Bartender enters, now wearing booty shorts and a tube crop top. Veratis is speechless and stunned by how amazing she looks.
Veratis speaks: You look incredible.
[Veratis asks the next question while signaling to his phone.]
Veratis speaks: I can take some pictures?
[MUSIC BEGINS TO PLAY]

[Bartender sits down, resting her butt against Veratis's thigh, as they both face the large mirror.]

[Bartender begins posing, cheek to cheek with Veratis, making kissy faces and throwing up a peace sign, while she rests her hand on Veratis's thigh.]

[Veratis begins to snap pictures, holding her stomach tightly with his left hand, while holding the camera with his right hand.]

[After a few snapshots, Bartender takes the camera from Veratis and continues to take pictures.]

[Veratis holds Bartender's stomach with both hands and play kisses her on the cheek as Bartender continues to snap photos.]

[Veratis and Bartender pose, making faces, while looking at each other through the mirror.]

[Bartender sticks out her tongue, and continues to take photos, as Veratis holds onto her waist.]
[The couple begins leaning to the side, almost falling off the bed.]

[With both of her feet on the ground, and her hands on the bed, Bartender leans over Veratis and puts her butt in the air while she looks at the mirror.]

[Veratis takes his camera-phone
and begins to record.]

[the song changes]
[Song comparable to first verse from "Tip Toes"]

[Song that plays is an opportunity for an up and
coming artist]

[Bartender begins to shake her bumbum to the music
while playfully looking back at the mirror.
[Veratis plays the role of her hype man.]
Veratis speaks: Shake that shit
Veratis speaks: Ay, Ay, Ay!

[Bartender adjusts her position, and continues to
jiggle her butt.]
Veratis speaks: Ay, Ay, Ay!
[Bartender lets out a cute small laugh]

[As Bartender shakes her bumbum, she leans on top
of Veratis and begins to kiss him as he lays down with
his back against the bed.]
[The camera falls down as the music plays, and we
no longer see the couple; we only hear the couple
kissing and enjoying each other's company.]

Bartender speaks loudly: It's so big!
Veratis speaks jokingly: I thought it was little
[Bartender lets out a cute laugh.]

[Camera slowly fades out]
[The scene ends]

[Scene 4]
Title: Bartender Wakes Up in Bed
Location: Bartender's Apartment
Length: 5 minutes

[Bartender wakes up in her bed.]
[Bartender stands up, using her blanket to cover herself.]

[Bartender begins to call for Veratis as she walks around her apartment looking for him.]

Bartender realizes… Veratis has left… in the middle of the night, while she was asleep.

[Next, we hear a phone's ringing tone.]
[Bartender is calling Veratis.]

[Veratis picks up.]
Veratis speaks via phone: Hey beautiful. Are you awake?
Bartender speaks via phone: Why did you leave?
Veratis speaks via phone: I didn't leave. I'm on your rooftop.
Bartender speaks via phone: You're on my rooftop?
Bartender speaks via phone: What are you doing?

Veratis speaks via phone: I came up here, to look at the stars.
Bartender speaks via phone: You are crazy. You know that?

Bartender speaks via phone: If you are really upstairs, you should come back to bed.

Veratis speaks via phone: No, not yet, I think you should come up here and hang out with me.

Bartender speaks via phone: I'm not walking upstairs Veratis.

Veratis speaks via phone: Well, what if I carry you upstairs?
[Bartender laughs]
Bartender speaks via phone: If you carry me upstairs, I will come up with you.
Veratis speaks via phone: Sounds like a challenge…. Give me one second. . .

[Scene changes within the scene]
[Bartender is looking at herself in her mirror. We hear the unlocking of a door.]

[Veratis enters.]

Veratis speaks: Your chariot awaits.

[The scene ends]

[Scene 5]
Title: Rooftop Lesson of the Stars
Location: Bartender's Rooftop
Length: 5 minutes

[We see Veratis carrying Bartender up the stairs; both of them laughing. Door opens and Veratis carries Bartender to a green lounge area with a wicker sofa and fireplace.]
Bartender speaks: That was so much fun!

[The night is magnificently lit up with stars.]

[Bartender and Veratis sit down, and Bartender snuggles up next to Veratis.]
Bartender speaks: What were you doing up here?
Veratis speaks: I just love to look at the stars.
Bartender speaks: Can I ask you something? But you can't get mad.
Veratis speaks: Go ahead.
Bartender speaks: Did you ever do anything like this with Twyla? Like, take her to a rooftop?
[Veratis answers kindly]
Veratis speaks: Wow, why would you ask that?
Bartender speaks: Well, last year, you were all she ever talked about. She would play your song "Homework," and talk about you all the time.

Veratis speaks: Just know— I do not talk to her anymore. She was super cool, no disrespect to her… but know… I am a single man.
Bartender speaks: I love your music also ya know.
Bartender speaks: I love your voice. It's even better in person.
Veratis speaks: Thanks.
[Veratis pauses, and then looks at Bartender and smiles.]
Veratis speaks: I love your smile.
Bartender speaks: Thank you.

[Veratis holds Bartender close and points to a bright white star in the sky. The star is clearly the brightest star in the sky.]

Veratis speaks: Do you see that star right there?
Bartender speaks: wow, it's so pretty. (Affirming that she sees the star)
Veratis speaks: It is not actually a star. That is the planet Jupiter.
Bartender speaks: How do you know?
[Veratis chuckles and then points to a bright red star that looks like a glowing red l.e.d. light, parked in the middle of the night sky]
Veratis speaks: do you see that really bright red star?
Bartender speaks: I've never seen a star glow like that.
Veratis speaks: That is the planet mars.
[Bartender looks at Veratis in awe, with a somewhat inquisitive look]
Bartender speaks: How do you know all of this?

Veratis speaks: I used to look at the stars, almost every night… and now I recognize them, like most people recognize the sun.

[Veratis pauses]

Veratis speaks: I think it is important that
we know the stars. I think that is the first step, in truly knowing where we are.

I'm not boring you am I?
Bartender speaks: No… I like it, I love your mind…

Veratis speaks: I won't bore you too much longer.
Veratis speaks: I will show you one more.

[Veratis points to the constellation Orion]
Veratis speaks: Do you see those stars?
Bartender speaks: Yes.
Veratis speaks: That is a picture of Har — the King…

Veratis speaks: In ancient Egypt, the kings believed that they, the kings, were the living manifestation of Har (Horus)… and that when they died… their souls would return to those stars…

[Veratis points to the top left star, of Orion]
Veratis speaks: Do you see that orange star?
Bartender speaks: Yeah.
Veratis speaks: That is his right hand.

[Veratis points to the top right star, of Orion]
Veratis speaks: You see that star?
Bartender speaks: the one a little to the right?
Veratis speaks: Yes.
Veratis speaks: That is his other hand.

[Veratis then points to the belt, of the constellation Orion]
Veratis speaks: Do you see those three stars?
Bartender speaks: I see them.
Veratis speaks: That is his belt.
Veratis speaks: You see his sword?
Bartender speaks: Oh wow, yeah, I see it. I've never looked at it like that.

Bartender speaks: So *those two are his feet?*

[Bartender points to the two bottom stars of Orion]
Veratis speaks: … exactly.

[Veratis points once again to the top left star, of
Orion]
So you see how his right hand looks orange?

Bartender speaks: Yes.

Veratis speaks: It was said that his right hand was the
Sun.

Veratis speaks: The ancients believed that God drew
a picture of himself in the sky, with the stars, and
that just like Horus held the sun, in order to see in
darkness, man too had to learn to hold fire.
We too have to learn to understand light.

Veratis speaks: In those days, the ability to melt and
refine Gold, was one of the ultimate masteries of fire,
for a king.

Veratis speaks: But today,

[The scene ends]

[Scene 6]
Title: The Next Morning
Location: Front of Bartender's House
Length: 5 minutes

[We hear, from the sounds of the city, that the time of day is morning.]

[Veratis exits the apartment building as a taxi pulls up.]
[Veratis enters into the taxi.]

[As the driver pulls off, he turns on the radio and lands mid-interview on an unknown radio station.]
Interviewer speaks via radio: Was there a moment that you realized that you were a star? when you realized that your talent, was unlike any of your contemporaries?

Unknown Celebrity speaks via radio: So my father always called me his "Heliacal Rising," while I was growing up, and I never really knew what it meant— "Heliacal Rising." I just knew that it had to do with the rising of a star.
My senior year of high school, we had a talent show…

[The interview comes to an abrupt end as the taxi driver turns down the volume and turns around.]

Taxi Driver speaks: Hey, is there anything you wanna to listen to? Any music you want me to play?

Veratis speaks: Naw, I'm cool. Whatever you play is fine with me.

[The taxi driver begins to search through music, scrolling through a large list of music on his dashboard, and chooses a song.]
[music begins to play]
[The scene ends]

[Scene 7]
Title: Veratis writes the Poem titled "Heliacal Rising"
Location: Veratis's Apartment
Length: 5 minutes

[Taxi driver pulls up to Veratis's apartment, and we see the red brick structure from outside.]

[We see Veratis's front door, from inside of his apartment.]

[Veratis unlocks the door, and the door swings open.] [We see Veratis is home.] [Veratis enters his apartment and walks with his backpack to his room. He sees his apartment is a mess. There are old pizza boxes and boxes of Chinese food on an island in the dining area directly behind the living room. No one seems to be home.]

Veratis goes down the hallway to a locked room on the right, and uses both a red key and a blue key to open the door. Veratis enters his room, and we see that Veratis's room is very clean and organized.

[Veratis sets down his backpack, and then exits the room. He goes into one of the apartment's restrooms and sees that it is riddled with mess. Veratis mumbles something under his breath.]
Veratis speaks: I can't fucking stand these fuckers!
Veratis leaves the restroom and finds the second restroom in his apartment. It is considerably smaller than the first restroom, but a bit cleaner.
[Veratis quickly brushes his teeth.]

Veratis walks back to his room and sits down at his desk. He removes his phone from his pocket and activates his phone's virtual assistant.

Veratis speaks: what is a "Heliacal Rising"?

[The virtual assistant takes a brief moment to process and then speaks.]

Virtual Assistant speaks via phone: "The heliacal rising of a star is a phenomena that can be seen along the eastern horizon during the rising of the sun each morning. Each month, a different star or group of stars becomes visible along the horizon, directly before sunrise. After 365 days, the same star or group of stars will return, once again, along the horizon. This annual occurrence was once used by different groups of ancient peoples as an early calendar. This observable pattern is often referred to as 'the precession of the stars.'"

[Veratis sits at his desk and thinks, and we begin to hear Veratis's thoughts as he begins to write.]

Veratis's thoughts:

Take a picture…
Just look over the horizon…
This is my
Heliacal Rising…
So,
I'm over your head…
Well…
That is not surprising…
But really…
I'm down to earth…
Even though…
I'm a super gi-ant…
And I love…
looking at myself…
On my phone…
Sky Maps…
Memorial-Lizing"

[We see a sheet of notebook paper, with the poem titled "Heliacal Rising," written out on his desk]

[The scene ends]

[Scene 8]
Title: First Day of Class, New School Year
Location: 101 Lecture Hall
Length: 5 minutes

It is Monday, and it is the first day of school. We see outside of the lecture hall. Students are out and about.

Visual cues suggest that the time of the day is morning. The Camera faces a lecture hall full of students, all seated, chattering, as they wait, for class to begin.

[The Camera faces the front of the lecture hall and is positioned behind the students.]

We see the backs of the students. We see that the professor has now entered and is at the front of the hall, preparing for the lecture to begin.

[The Camera focuses in on the professor.]

Teacher speaks: Good morning students.

[The students begin to quiet down.]

Teacher speaks: I am your professor— Professor Nkwo Achi

[The teacher speaks with a thick African accent that captivates the room.]

Teacher speaks: Each of you should have your Syllabus, and all the required books.

Teacher speaks: And hopefully— have all brought an apparatus for taking notes.

Teacher speaks: I will start this semester off, by saying— My hope for each and every one of you — is that— when you leave this class, at the end of this semester, you each have an understanding— *of the courage that it takes to be great.*

[We watch as the class listens attentively.]

Teacher speaks: Are any of you great?—
Teacher speaks: That is a rhetorical question, but I want each and every one of you to think. I want each of you to do an analysis of yourselves.

Teacher speaks: Are you great? Do you have greatness inside of you?

Teacher speaks: Unfortunately, fearlessness is not something that can easily be taught. But— understanding… that many of the greats were also once afraid— is something that can be learned.

[We see the class attentively listening as the professor moves around the class.]

Teacher speaks: You cannot afford to be afraid. You cannot be afraid to think differently than your peers. You do not have the time to think small. It takes courage to suggest a better solution. It takes courage, to dream beyond the stars.

That is, what this class is all about.

Teacher speaks: If you think—that you already think big, I want you to start thinking even bigger.

Teacher speaks: Greatness… is when the people who live thousands of years from now, thank the heavens that you lived."

[The scene ends]

[Scene 9]
Title: Nicholas gives Veratis a Beats CD
Location: Outside of Class, on sidewalk
Length: 5 minutes

[We see a large mass of students exiting the lecture hall. Veratis emerges from the crowd walking down the sidewalk.]

[We see campus signage, which gives us the feeling of a college campus.]

Nicholas speaks: Hey!!!!!!!!!!!!!!!!!! Kpakpando! ! !
[Veratis senses that someone may be calling him, but continues walking.]

Nicholas speaks: Veratis!!!!!!!!!!!!!!
[Veratis hears his name being called, and turns around. We see Nicholas Santos running to catch up to Veratis.]

[Nicholas, out of breath, catches up to Veratis.]

Nicholas speaks: Hey. You are Veratis right?
Veratis speaks: Can I help you? (With a questioning look on his face)

Nicholas speaks: I heard you on the radio last year.
That verse you did was dope…

Veratis speaks: I'm not exactly sure what verse I did?
but… thank you?

Nicholas speaks: I'm not trying to be weird or
anything, but you should take my CD.

[Veratis looks at Nicholas somewhat confused]
[Nicholas goes into his backpack and pulls out a
compact disc.]

Nicholas speaks: You should write something to one
of my beats. I started making music again last year,
because of your music. That New York Remix
that you had online…. I actually learn things from
your music.

Veratis speaks: I appreciate it man.

[Nicholas hands Veratis the compact disc.]
Nicholas speaks: You should write a song to one of my
beats.

[Veratis accepts the CD and puts it in his backpack]
Veratis speaks: I cannot promise anything, but I can
take a listen.
Nicholas speaks: that's all I ask.

[The Scene Ends]

[Scene 10]
Title: Veratis and Bartender have dinner
Location: Restaurant
Length: 5 minutes

[We see a cozy restaurant on the corner of a campus street. Veratis is seated inside of the restaurant. His clothing is different from the previous scene because we have advanced an unknown amount of time.]

[Veratis is waiting for Bartender, as they have agreed to meet for dinner.]

[Bartender walks in and walks over to Veratis and takes a seat on the opposite side of the table.]

Bartender speaks: I got here as soon as I could, I just got out of a meeting with my guidance counselor.

Veratis speaks: I hope it went well.
Bartender speaks: It did go well.

Veratis speaks: Good to hear! are you hungry?
Bartender speaks: I'm starving. Thank you.

Veratis speaks: Well… get whatever you like.

[Bartender looks at Veratis and smiles because Veratis is being quite the gentleman.]
Bartender speaks: Why thank you.

Veratis speaks: How has your day been?
Bartender speaks: My day has been okay. Ya know. One month of school— and I'm ready to drop out. [Bartender says the end of her sentence somewhat sarcastically.]

Veratis looks at Bartender— using his facial expression to tell her that she better not be serious.

Veratis speaks: Well, I won't allow that to happen.
Bartender speaks: Awe…
Bartender speaks: Thanks.

Bartender speaks: The meeting I just had with my guidance counselor.
Bartender speaks: I want to drop my Political Science class. My professor— I'm either going to have to kill her with kindness— or— I'm just going to have to kill her. And the latter… is not going to help me get into law school.

[Veratis laughs]

Veratis speaks: I didn't know you wanted to go to law school?
Bartender speaks: Yeah.

Veratis speaks: Do you know what type of law you want to go into?
Bartender speaks: I don't know yet. I just know I want to help people who don't have the money to afford traditional lawyers.

Bartender speaks: I see how money controls so much of our society. I don't think it is right. So I want to provide affordable legal services.

[Veratis looks at Bartender with a surprised face]

Veratis speaks: Wow. That's impressive.
Veratis speaks: So why do you want to drop your
political science class?

Bartender speaks: It's just my professor is the worst.
She literally does not know how to teach. She must
just love to hear the sound of her own voice because
nobody in the class knows what she is talking about.
[Bartender pauses]
Bartender speaks: And… because there is this dance
class being taught by Nicole K. And it's just this
semester— this semester only.
Bartender speaks: And she is a legend. She has done
choreography for everyone.

[Veratis looks at Bartender]
Veratis speaks: You want to dance?

Bartender speaks: Her class is already filled up.
Bartender speaks: . . . and… it's at the same time as my
political science class. But it's already filled up.

Veratis speaks: You have to talk to her! Show up
to class, wait until it's over, and talk to her.

Bartender speaks: Do you think that could work?
Veratis speaks: Yes!!! Make it happen!!!

Bartender speaks: Wow, thank you so much. I needed to hear that.

Bartender speaks: I'm going to talk to her. Thank you Veratis.

[Bartender pauses]
Bartender speaks: That reminds me. A few weeks ago, you told me that your friend gave you a beat CD or usb. Have you made any new music?

Veratis speaks: First off.. He is not my friend.
Veratis speaks: He is a kid who is trying to woo me into recording on some of his beats.

[Bartender laughs]

Bartender speaks: Veratis, he's not woo'ing you. You have a talent.

Veratis speaks: Okay, then why did he invite me to his apartment to play video games?
[Veratis says the line jokingly]

[Bartender laughs]

Veratis speaks: And… he lives at The Plex.
Bartender speaks: Woah? The Plex? Isn't that the apartment for the rich kids?

Veratis speaks: Well….
Veratis speaks: It's just got a beach volleyball court, basketball court, golf simulator, piano room, pool on the roof, but…… who's counting?

[Bartender laughs]

Bartender speaks: Veratis, there's nothing wrong with making new friends. College…. is all about meeting new people…. The whole world comes to you. Instead of you having to travel the whole world in search of a beat maker.

Veratis speaks: To be honest— I just haven't had much time.

Bartender speaks: I think you need a little bit of your own advice today….
Bartender speaks: Make it happen!
Bartender speaks: In my Lit. class today, we were breaking down the verses of one of my favorite poets.

Bartender speaks:

How could you have a dream—
and not chase it—
Have a chance
and not take it—
Have a passion
— not make it—
Into what you do,
every day—
You better catch that bird
Before it flies away—
Or you might have some regrets—
On your dying day.

[The Scene Ends]
[Bartenders words continue into the next scene]

[Scene 11]
Title: Veratis writes "One Day I'ma Be A Star"
Location: Veratis's Apartment
Length: 5 minutes

[Scene starts with ["Never Let Them Take Your Voice"]
[Mellow Mood Instrumental] playing.]

[Veratis begins to play music on his stereo system,
although, to the viewer, the music is already playing.]

[Veratis presses the record button on his phone, and
takes out a notepad and pen from his backpack.]

[He begins writing to the music, and we watch as he
walks about his apartment.]

[After writing a few words down on his notepad,
he tears out a sheet of paper from the notepad and
crumples it up.]

[We see fast speed footage of the city and others in
Veratis's life, i.e. Bartender and Nicholas as the music
continues to play.]

[Veratis then stops the music.]

[Veratis presses the forward button to play the next instrumental.]

[The second beat begins to play.]
["One Day I'ma Be A Star" Instrumental begins to play.]

[The second beat is rich and dramatic, and begins to move Veratis to start a freestyle.]

[Veratis immediately becomes entranced by the music… and begins saying, "One day I'ma be a star" "One day I'ma be a star" to the beat.]

["One Day I'ma Be A Star" instrumental plays]

Veratis speaks:
One day I'ma be a star...
One day I'ma be a star...
I'ma Be a Star...

One day I'ma be a star...
One day I'ma be a star...
I'ma Be a Star...

One day I'ma be a star...
One day I'ma be a star...
I'ma Be a Star...

I'ma Be...
I'ma Be...
I'ma Be...
I'ma Be...
I'ma Be...
I'ma Be A Star...
I'ma Be A Star...

[the beat drops]

Veratis raps:
Examine my d%&...
You'll find star quality...
Fuck you, pay me...
No apologies...
Cause I was fucking broke...
No fucking hope...
No fucking help...
No fucking smoke...
Now I feel like...
burning all y'all...
Cause the fire inside me...
Cannot be controlled y'all...
Bang bang...
Lights out...
Blackhole y'all...
Y'all don't even know...
Where the hell you're bout to go y'all...
But me, I got a place in The Sky
Cousin...
So I'ma live there for eternity...
And I don't need to go on Maury...
To become a star...
No
I don't need your paternity...
Cause even the sperm in me...
Know the words to this f'n hook...
Boy, you look just like your damn daddy...
Look up...
take another fucking look...

One day I'ma be a star…
One day I'ma be a star…
I'ma Be a Star…

One day I'ma be a star…
One day I'ma be a star…
I'ma Be a Star…

One day I'ma be a star…
One day I'ma be a star…
I'ma Be a Star…

I'ma Be…
I'ma Be…
I'ma Be…
I'ma Be…
I'ma Be…
I'ma Be A Star…
I'ma Be A Star…

[the beat drops]
Veratis begins to rap a second verse:

Stars…
Cowboys…
Texas Rangers…
Big titty chicks…
That say hello to strangers…
But I got a CD,
So she thinks she knows me…
Hydrogen…
Helium…
Told the bitch to blow me…
I pull hoes…
Call it gravitation…
You pull nothing…
Call it masturbation…
With these hoes,
no procrastination…
Shit I hit the first night…
Then it's back to chasin…
The shit that makes the world go round…
Yeahhhhh…
The shit that makes your girl go down…
Yeahhhhh…
And she said that she likes the beat…
Said my niggas look like stars…
And wants to ride with a G…
And that ass…
It was astronomical…
Copernicus…
Could not guess what I'ma do…
cause… everyday… a star is born…
So… that's what I'ma do.

Veratis speaks:
One day I'ma be a star...
One day I'ma be a star...
I'ma Be a Star...

One day I'ma be a star...
One day I'ma be a star...
I'ma Be a Star...

One day I'ma be a star...
One day I'ma be a star...
I'ma Be a Star...

I'ma Be...
I'ma Be...
I'ma Be...
I'ma Be...
I'ma Be...
I'ma Be A Star...
I'ma Be A Star...

[Veratis forgets that he is still recording.]
[We see a view of Veratis's phone, and see that
his phone is still recording]
[The Scene Ends]

[Scene 12]
Title: Class Scene Number Two
Location: 101 Lecture Hall

[students listen attentively to the professor as he
speaks]

Teacher speaks:
Before I won my first Nobel prize, I was just like you.

I remember looking at []Magazine's most influential
people— and at my country's currency— and asking
myself, "if these faces represented. . . what it meant to
dream?"

I remember myself as a college student the year
before I graduated… I stood in front of the mirror,
and I asked myself, "Who am I?"

It was in those moments… that I realized…. that just
as it is important…. to know where you are…. it is just
as important…. to know where you are going.

Many of you… could not get to your destination
without GPS… but there is no GPS in real life.

Mentors, teachers, and people with great experience,
often serve as guides.

But. . . the purpose of college— is for you to learn
to think for yourself. And when it is all said and done,
if you have not learned that, then you have not learned
anything.

[The Scene Ends]

[Scene 13]
Title: Veratis shows song to Beatmaker
Location: Nicholas's Apartment
Length: 5 minutes

[Nicholas and two friends, Polo and Strobush, are
playing video games and having a friendly debate at
Nicholas's apartment.]

Nicholas speaks: Neverrrrrrrrrrrrrrrr. You are not
all there. He can never be the goat. MJ is the greatest
of all time. You clearly didn't have older siblings to
school you to the game. The only way that your boy
could ever be the goat, is if he undergoes a sex change,
and joins the W league, and then plays another ten
years as a woman, and wins a couple championships…
Then…. You can call him the goat.

Polo speaks: Damnnnnnnnn, you gonna do my boy
like that? You're crazy.

Strobush speaks: Nick does have a point tho. MJ won
three straight, left the league, and had the whole world
waiting for him to come back, wishing on the stars
for him to return….

Then he came back, and did it again, one year, after
another year, after another year.
He had the world's attention for eight straight years.
It was poetic.

[Polo speaks sarcastically]
Polo speaks: Man………
Polo speaks: fuck y'all.

[Doorbell Rings]

[Nicholas presses intercom]
Nicholas speaks: Who is it?
Veratis speaks: it's Veratis
[Nicholas presses button to open building door]

[Time moves forward]
[We here a knock on the Door]

Nicholas speaks: Its Open!
[Veratis enters.]
Nicholas speaks: You finally decided to come
through?
Veratis speaks: Yeah…
Nicholas speaks: Make yourself at home.

Nicholas speaks: Polo, this is Veratis. Veratis, this is
Polo, he lives down the hall.
[The two gentlemen greet each other.]

[Nicholas then motions toward his other friend]
Nicholas speaks: and this is Strobush. Strobush, this is
Veratis.
[The two nod, and say "what's up," acknowledging one
another.]
Nicholas speaks: You listen to any of those beats?
Veratis speaks: Yeah. I was looking for you in class.
Nicholas speaks: Yeah, I didn't go to class today.

Nicholas speaks: But what'd you think?

Veratis speaks: They were dope.
[Veratis pauses]

Veratis speaks: last night I was recording with my
voice notes… and it was like… the song just came to
me.
Veratis speaks: I just started saying, "One day I'ma be
a star, One day I'ma be a star."

Nicholas speaks: what type of phone do you have?
[Veratis takes out his phone]
[The two connect his phone to the speaker]
[Veratis begins to play "One Day I'ma Be A Star"]
[and turns up the volume]

[Veratis speaks via the recording:]
One day I'ma be a star…
One day I'ma be a star…
I'ma Be a Star…

One day I'ma be a star…
One day I'ma be a star…
I'ma Be a Star…

One day I'ma be a star…
One day I'ma be a star…
I'ma Be a Star…

I'ma Be…
I'ma Be…
I'ma Be…
I'ma Be…
I'ma Be…
I'ma Be A Star…
I'ma Be A Star…

Veratis raps via recording:

Examine my dick…
You'll find star quality…
Fuck you, pay me…
No apologies…
Cause I was fucking broke…
No fucking hope…
No fucking help…
No fucking smoke…
Now I feel like burning all y'all…
Cause the fire inside me…
Cannot be controlled y'all…
Bang bang…
Lights out…
Blackhole y'all…
Y'all don't even know…
Where the hell
you're bout to go y'all…
But me I got a place in the sky
Cousin…
So I'ma live there for eternity…
And I don't need to go on Maury…
To become a star…
No, I don't need your paternity…
Cause even the sperm in me…
Know the words
to this f'n hook…
Boy you look just like your damn daddy…
Look up…
take another fucking look…

One day I'ma be a star…
One day I'ma be a star…
I'ma Be a Star…

One day I'ma be a star…
One day I'ma be a star…
I'ma Be a Star…

One day I'ma be a star…
One day I'ma be a star…
I'ma Be a Star…

I'ma Be…
I'ma Be…
I'ma Be…
I'ma Be…
I'ma Be…
I'ma Be A Star…
I'ma Be A Star…

Veratis raps via recording:

Stars…
Cowboys…
Texas Rangers…
Big titty chicks…
That say hello to strangers…
But I got a CD,
So she thinks she knows me…
Hydrogen…
Helium…
Told the bitch to blow me…
I pull hoes…
Call it gravitation…
You pull nothing…
Call it masturbation…
With these hoes,
no procrastination…
Shit I hit the first night…
Then it's back to chasin…
The shit that makes the world go round…
Yeahhhhh…
The shit that makes your girl go down…
Yeahhhhh…
And she said that she likes the beat…
Said my niggas look like stars…
And wants to ride with a G…
And that ass…
It was astronomical…
Copernicus…
Could not guess what I'ma do…
cause… everyday… a star is born…
So… that's what I'ma do.

One day I'ma be a star...
One day I'ma be a star...
I'ma Be a Star...

One day I'ma be a star...
One day I'ma be a star...
I'ma Be a Star...

One day I'ma be a star...
One day I'ma be a star...
I'ma Be a Star...

I'ma Be...
I'ma Be...
I'ma Be...
I'ma Be...
I'ma Be...
I'ma Be A Star...
I'ma Be A Star...

[While the song is playing, Nicholas and Polo look at
each other, affirming that they like the song.]
[The song finishes]

Polo speaks: That shit was dope!
Polo speaks: Stars, Cowboys, Texas Rangers, big titty chicks, that say hello to strangers!

Veratis speaks: I appreciate it.

Veratis speaks: Just know, "G" does not mean organized crime member.

Veratis speaks: Gangster means paperchaser, who doesn't involve himself in things he can't handle. Because if real really recognizes real…. Why are all these guys getting snitched on?

Smart recognizes smart.

Nicholas speaks: That's why I fuck with you Veratis.

Veratis speaks: My dad was shot during the Nigerian Biafran war, and two of my uncles were killed.
They fought for the freedom of their people.
That is gangster to me.

[Nicholas looks on with an informed look]

Veratis speaks: I have to be the education for my people.

Veratis speaks: We have to return to the days when someone could sing, "I shot the sheriff," and no one would actually try to shoot the sheriff.
[The Scene Ends]

[Scene 14]
Title: Bartender's Dance Class
Location: Dance Studio
Length: 5 minutes

[The scene starts off with Music playing]
[We see a dance class is going on. Bartender is one of
the students in the class. The instructor tells the class
to take a break.]

[During the break, Bartender goes to check her phone,
and we see a message from Veratis telling her to come
outside]

[We see Veratis is outside of the class, waiting with a
rose.]
[Bartender goes outside]

Bartender speaks: Hey you.
Veratis speaks: I have something for you.
[Veratis pulls out a rose from inside of his shirt, and
hands it to Bartender.]
Bartender speaks: Oh wow, thank you.

[We see some of Bartender's female classmates
watching Bartender & Veratis from the window.]

[Bartender accepts the rose, and is smitten with
Veratis and his gesture.]
Veratis speaks: I just wanted to come and see you
and say thank you…. what you said to me the other
day. I needed that.

Bartender speaks: No really, thank you Veratis.
I spoke to Nicole, and she let me in her class.
I would not have been here if it wasn't for you.

Veratis speaks: Well, you just gotta show me some of those dance moves…. later.
Bartender speaks: Okay, I will.

Bartender speaks: There's actually one move that I want you to work with me on.

Veratis speaks: Sounds like a plan
[Veratis and Bartender look at each other.]
[Bartender takes a deep breath and gathers herself.]

Bartender speaks: Today, Nicole told us about a competition in New York, for musicians.
The grand prize is $100,000.

Bartender speaks: We've all heard you Veratis. Even some of my classmates know who you are.

Veratis speaks: What? You think I should enter?
Bartender speaks: Yes.
[Veratis pauses]
Veratis speaks: It's 100,000 dollars? ?
Bartender speaks: Yes.
Veratis speaks: I will look it up, and I will call you tonight.

Bartender speaks: Okay.
Bartender speaks: I'll be waiting.
Veratis speaks: I'll let you hear my new song.
Bartender speaks: Okay. I can't wait.

[The scene ends]

[Scene 15]
Title: "The Beloved Triangle"
Location: Bartender's & Veratis's Respective Apartments
Length: 5 minutes

[Bartender lays on her bed, with her phone next to her on speaker phone.]
[Veratis lays on his bed, at his own apartment..]
[Both are awake and enjoying their four-hour-long conversation.]

Veratis speaks: remember how we looked up at the constellation "Horus" that night?
Bartender speaks: Yeah, I will always remember.

Veratis speaks: Remember how I showed you the hand that holds the sun?
Bartender speaks: Yeah.

Veratis speaks: That hand makes a perfect triangle with two stars to the left of it.

Veratis speaks: I left a book at your place.

Bartender speaks: Yeah, I saw it the other day. I set it on my night stand.
[Bartender reaches over and collects the book off of her night stand.]
Bartender speaks: I have it right here.

Veratis speaks: Look at the cover.
Veratis speaks: You see the star on the bottom left?
Bartender speaks: Yes.

Veratis speaks: That star, today, is known as Sirius.

Veratis speaks: You see the star on the top left?
Veratis speaks: You see how the stars make a perfect equilateral triangle?
Bartender speaks: Yeah.

Veratis speaks: That is, "The Beloved Triangle."

Veratis speaks: the star on the bottom left— which is now known as "Sirius"— was once known as the wife of Horus.[1]

Veratis speaks: the top left star, was known as "the newborn king"— the child who would one day become king.

Veratis speaks: The Father, the Mother, and the newborn king— a holy Trinity— of that time.

Bartender speaks: I like how you tell that story.

[1] also known as "crown of the wife of Horus"

Veratis speaks: Princes and princesses back then were taught, that they themselves were the "newborn king."

And that the triangle, was a picture, written by God, of them looking at the stars.

Veratis speaks: So in life, they too had to go out and look at the stars, to fulfill what was written by God.

Bartender speaks: That is beautiful.

Veratis speaks: Yeah.

Veratis speaks: The book I'm reading though— says— the top left star is actually two stars— so close together that we see them as one.

So, now, the top left star will represent the old and the new. The old— being the newborn king, and the new— being— a boy and girl, both rulers, looking up at the stars.

Bartender speaks: So this star is like us… the night we were looking up at the stars?
Veratis speaks: Yeah.
[Pause]

Bartender speaks: Do you want to come over and have sex?
[Veratis looks at the camera and smiles.]

Veratis speaks: I'll be over in 15 minutes.

[The scene ends]

[Two Months Later]

SCENE 16 -
VERATIS RECEIVES ACCEPTANCE LETTER
Veratis receives acceptance letter to RSVP New York,
the music competition in New York.

SCENE 17 -
FLIGHT TO NEW YORK
Orchestral / Epic Music Plays
We see an airplane flying through the air, and we infer
that Veratis is flying to New York for a possible life
changing moment.

SCENE 18 -
AIRPORT SCENE
Veratis stops to get a rental car in the airport.
[This is a sponsor opportunity.]
OR—Veratis stops at a barber shop in The Bronx,
to cut his hair.
[The scene ends]

These scenes were reduced for a smoother reading experience. Readers,
imagine all the different scene possiblities, between Scene 15 - and this page.

[Scene 19]
Title: RSVP New York - Day One
$100,000 Prize Competition Day One
Location: Madison Square Garden
Length: 5 minutes

[Camera is rolling, nationwide broadcast is being recorded live.]

Announcer 1: We are here at RSVP New York. Today twenty-five lucky contestants have earned their way to an all expenses paid trip to Manhattan.

Each contestant submitted a video of themselves to our panel, performing one of their best songs, and one song only. Each contestant was then hand picked by our panel of judges to be flown here to Manhattan, for the opportunity of a lifetime. A chance to win $100,000, and a possible record contract.

Announcer 2: That is— life changing money— for some of our contestants.

Announcer 1: You bet it is Announcer 2, some of these contestants have been singing the blues in their real lives, and now, regardless of their situation, they're going to have to turn all of those emotions, into powerful energy, that will make them unforgettable to our judges.

Announcer 2: You're right Announcer 1, the first round is all about lyrics though— word play. The first round, is the Acapella Round. Here, each contestant will perform their song with no beat. No music at all. That way, the Judges get to see each artist in raw form, and cannot be enticed by anything else besides the artist themselves.

Announcer 1: Today we have nine amazing ladies performing, along with sixteen young men. But who will be the most captivating? Who's delivery and stage presence will be unforgettable?

Announcer 2: We will find out tomorrow, because that's when these judges will cast their votes to reveal who will be— the five— "Rap Stars Vying for Power." Only five contestants will receive an RSVP— an invitation to perform on tomorrow's final grand stage.

So let's go down to the Main Stage because it looks like the competition is underway.

[The Camera changes]

Male Artist raps:
I was everything you wanted…
There was never anything you needed…
I was the first nigga to run up in it…
The first to make you bleed…
You lost your virginity to me…
Now you're begging me not to leave…
I aint blind…
But its a g% damn shame…
That I needed my friends eyes just to see…
That you stabbed me in the back…
While standing in front of me…
I thought that could never happen…
Never mind the questions…
Get the fuck away from me…
Better never say accident…
Let me ask you bitch…
Did you trip on his fucking dick?
After your mouth was up on his lips?
Or before you let him all up in my crib?
Shit…
I couldn't even fathom that happening…
Because you fell for me first…
I was the one that should have left you…
Crying all up in the hurts…
The one that should have left you pregnant…
Just to give up or give birth…
The one that should have left you bad…
When you was doing your worst…
But I didn't…
So yeah…
I'm glad you're sad and regret it…
And everything I said,
like I hate you…
Yes I fucking meant it…
(cont.)

I said I loved you girl…
You were the only girl that heard I said it…
So I'm never gonn' forgive you…
Even if I could forget it…

[Artist begins to say the hook]

(Hook)
Girl you better
Never…
Stop…
Never…
Sleep…
Never…
Talk…
Never…
Speak…
Never…
Lie…
Never…
Cheat…
They say Never Say Never…
But if we're in this together….
You Better Never…

[During the hook, the scene fades into the next scene
with the next artist]

[Next Artist]
[Gorgeous Latina Female Rapper]

Gorgeous Latina Rapper speaks:
Nigga you wasn't even there…
I had to grow up…
Thinking that you didn't care…
You never played with me…
So I became a player…
I only wanted your eyes…
Now every nigga stares…
Yeah
life ain't fair…
Still…
my heart tears…
Going to school
All the other girls
Had their daddies…
Picking them up…
Now I got blunts in my hands…
Bad habits…
I'm picking 'em up…
(cont.)

Now my…

Momma's yelling…
"You'll be a felon"…
Is she tripping or what?…
Now…
I'm selling…
You want it raw? …
I gave it to 'em…
uncut…
But still you split…
Got your chips and dipped…
And left me broken…
My whole life…
No dad on my side…
Showing me how to ride…
Telling me…
To hold tight…
And I
Still got that scar…
From when I fell…
And scraped my knee…
So if you…
Know the words
to this song…
I'll pray for you…
If you pray for me….

[Scene changes to the next artist]

[Nigerian Male Reggae Artist]

Nigerian Male Reggae Artist Sings:
She…..
made it all the way…
To the west side of town…
She didn't have a car…
So I don't even know
how…
I think she's getting getting getting getting…
Down…
Down down down…
Down down down…
Down down…
****

She get around cause she get around…
She get around cause she get around…
She get around cause she…
If you could see…
How she moves around…
By hitting half the town…
Then nna proof would be…
But I don't blame her…
Oh no, she never knew…
Nobody taught her…
Think we…
Maybe… blessed are you…
She get around cause she get around…
She get around cause she get around…
She get around cause she…
She get around cause she get around…
She get around cause she get around…
She get around cause she…

[Veratis's phone begins to vibrate]
[To the viewer, the vibration is louder than the Reggae singer's audition.]
[We see on Veratis's phone, that it is Bartender calling]

[Veratis answers his phone, while walking away from the viewing area to take the call]

Veratis speaks: Hey babe?
Bartender speaks: Hey
Veratis speaks: Just give me one second.
Bartender speaks: No problem (she says with a smile)

[Veratis exits the viewing area]

Veratis speaks: how are you beautiful?
Bartender speaks: I'm good, How are you Mr. RSVP, How is the event going? did you perform?
Veratis speaks: Not yet, probably won't for a couple hours. Everything just started, and I'm one of the last to perform.
Bartender speaks: Well, still, that is exciting. I wish I was there. I'll be praying for you. And thinking about you. Just keep those rap star girls off you.
[Veratis laughs]
Veratis speaks: Okay I will.

Bartender speaks: Okay... well I will get back to work. Me and some of the girls are at my place working on a new dance routine.

[We see Bartender and her classmates Esther and Katrina.]

Veratis speaks: Okay. You girls have fun.
Bartender speaks: Take care of yourself.
Veratis speaks: I will. You too.
Bartender speaks: Ok we'll talk later.
Veratis speaks: Okay. Later babe.

[Veratis re-enters the viewing area, and a new contestant is about to perform.]
[The scene ends]

[Scene 20]
Title: Relaxing after Competition Day 1
Location: New York Hotel
Length: 5 minutes

[Veratis and Nicholas are relaxing in their two-bed luxury hotel room after day one of the competition.]

[All other contestants are in the same hotel.]

Veratis speaks: How the hell am I supposed to sleep, when I know there's a $100,000 dollar bag on the line?

Veratis speaks: Tomorrow, whether we win or lose, we are going out to the club.
Nicholas speaks: Sounds good to me. Did you see that fine ass hispanic girl?

Veratis speaks: Yeah. Her song was dope. "Forever Scars."

Nicholas speaks: Yeah, did you see she's from Texas too?

Veratis speaks: You should get her info.
Veratis speaks: She definitely has that "it" factor.

Veratis speaks: Did you hear that guy from. . . I'm forgetting where he's from.

Veratis speaks: His song was hard—
That niggas a G, that niggas a hustler
cause hustlers make money by the G nigga.
That niggas a G, that niggas a hustler
cause gangsters make money by the hustle nigga.

Nicholas speaks: Yeah. That was dope.

Veratis speaks:
He said…
Watch out…
I mean watch my moves…
Selling cd's like weed…
That's what you do…
If they want…
Sixteen ounces…
Give em sixteen measures…
Yeah…
sixteen bars…
Is sixteen measures…
You see…
Each verse…
I spit
Is a whole pound…
See I don't break it down…
But let me break it down….

[Veratis shakes his head in amazement]

Vertatis speaks:
I forget what he said after that
But he started doing that math. Yeah that was dope.

Veratis speaks: But I don't know if the judges even
realized how hard he snapped. Because they seemed
confused.
[Veratis laughs]

Veratis speaks: That's why I don't like these
competitions… because who are these judges?

Veratis speaks: How do we even know they're qualified
to judge? Or they're not just getting paid off?

If this competition was for $1000, I wouldn't do it. But
for $100,000, I had no choice.

Nicholas speaks: All I know—
is you snapped today—
& that Mexican girl is fucking hot.

Veratis speaks: How you know she's Mexican?
Nicholas speaks: I don't. The hispanic girl.

Nicholas speaks: but really, there were a lot of
good performers today. We just have to wait until
tomorrow. It really just depends on who's voting.

Veratis speaks: True.

[Veratis lays his head down on his pillow.]
Veratis speaks: I'm going to sleep.

[The scene ends]

[Scene 21]
Title: Dallas Dance Studio
Location: Dallas Dance Studio
Length: 5 minutes

[Sometimes We Take Instrumental] Plays softly in the background
[Instrumental = Beat with no words]

[Bartender and some of her classmates have a dance practice, for a new routine they are working on, outside of class.]

[We see Bartender and her friends Esther and Katrina practicing.]

[Scene 22]
Title: Competition Day Two
Location: Madison Square Garden
Length: 5 minutes

Announcer 1: Today we have twenty-five of the hottest aspiring musicians from across the country. But only 5 of them will be advancing today.

And of those 5 contestants, each of them will be performing today, but only one of them— will be leaving here with $100,000 cash.

And. . . in addition to that large sum, he or she will be leaving here with three months paid studio time, at one of New York's finest studios. And, a chance to secure a record deal.

Announcer 2: That is true Announcer 1, but no contestant will be leaving here empty handed… Each contestant will leave here with exposure unlike any other…, as todays events are being broadcast on streaming sites all around the world… And… all 5 contestants who advance to the next round will leave here with a minimum $2,500 consolation prize.

Announcer 1: All of our runners-up will also leave here with an increased sense of hunger— the hunger to hone their craft and come back even stronger because true champions— never give up.

Today we have twenty-five stars vying for power, and they all have aligned here on this day. So who will shine the brightest? That is the question. So, with no further adieu, let's take it to our host.

[Host speaking to the audience]

Host speaks:
Hello everyone,
Welcome to RSVP New York Day Two!
Yesterday's performances were amazing.

[Host looks at the 25 performers]
Host speaks: You were all amazing, and every one of
you should be proud for all the hard work you put in
to get to this point.
In just a few moments though, we will be calling five
names, each of which will be receiving a check for
$2,500!

If you receive your check, just know $100,000 is on
the line.

Host speaks: Do you want to keep your $2,500
check? Or— do you want to exchange that check for
$100,000 dollars? That is the question.

So— remember— give the performance of your life—
and don't hold back.

If your name is called, come up and accept your
check… You will give your performance. . .
and after performing, you will take your seat *at the
Star Table.*

[Suspenseful music begins to play]

[host begins to speak in a loud broadcaster voice.]

The first contestant who will be performing today, is hailing all the way from 8 Mile Detroit.

He performed his song titled "Company Man" yesterday, but today he has chosen to perform an entirely different song titled, "I Don't Like You."

With no further adieu, come on up to the Star Table, "Mighty Medieval!"

[The audience and the other contestants clap as the contestant stands up and hurries up to the stage.]

[Mighty Medieval is a slender caucasian male with a shaved very short haircut, bleach blonde hair, and blue eyes.]

[Host speaks to Mighty Medieval]
Host speaks: So, Mighty Medieval, how did you get your name:
Mighty Medieval speaks: So really, as you can see from my lyrics, I have some old fashioned views. I feel like, my soul is really not from this time period. Right now is a volatile time in the United States. You got men trying to play in women's sports, and I'm not with none of that shit.

Host speaks: Okay (attempting to cut Mighty Medieval off before he says anything more.) Well, thank you for your answer. You will be performing first, and the judges are anxious to hear your second performance.

Host speaks: Not trying to put any pressure on you, but $100,000 is on the line.

[Host hands a microphone to Mighty Medieval]
Host speaks: DJ, drop the beat!

[Mighty Medieval hears the music, and with the microphone in one hand, he begins to perform]

[Music begins to play. The beat sounds amazing.]
[after about four seconds, Mighty Medieval begins to rap his song.]

Mighty Medieval raps:
I Don't like you…
I want you to leave…
You make me
want to go home…
and fucking beat my meat…
Biatch.
Bitch I Don't like you…
I want you to leave…
You make me want to go home…
and fucking beat my meat…

Mighty Medieval raps:
Bitch, you got a pretty face…
an ugly attitude…
%#&, your attitude…
determines your latitude…
show some fucking gratitude…
Ain't got no manners…
Rude…
You think you run shit…
doing shit
a man'll do…
This ain't no aptitude…
This ain't no fucking test…
these are testicles…
On your fucking breasts…
Now fucking make a mess…
And then go clean it up…
And after that %#&…
Go and cook me something…
No matter of fact…
Clean up the whole house…
%#& close your mouth…
Naw you ain't goin out…
Not dressed like that…
Looking like a hoe…
I thought I'd let you know…
I fuck— and let 'em go…
Out to the track
If you want to be a tracklete…

I need a smart bitch
With a good brain
A mathlete…
Not a %#&
that's addicted to them athletes…
Addicted to the dick…
Cause I beat it like an athlete…

And the sex
is a professional sport…
The bed
is my professional court…
You are a…
professional
whore…
You say you're not going out
dressed like a whore?
But you're dressed
like a whore…
And that's cool
if you're just one of my
be'itches…
bitches with good credit
Need to pay attention…
But…
To be my main chiiickkk…
You gotta keep that ass up in the kitchen!

[The whole crowd goes crazy, as they cannot believe
what they just heard]

Mighty Medieval raps:
Bitch I Don't like you…
I want you to leave…
You make me
want to go home…
and fucking beat my meat…
Biatch. . .
Bitch I Don't like you…
I want you to leave…
You make me want to go home…
and fucking beat my meat…
Biiitch.

[Scene changes within the scene]

Host speaks: Wow. That was quite the song. That's gotta be a tough act to follow.

Host speaks: Well, I had the opportunity to speak with our next contestant yesterday, and he told me that he ain't got no worries. He performed his song with no beat yesterday and mesmerized judges.

In his city... he hails from Uptown... but today. . .
we had to have him come and say hello
to downtown Manhattan.

Host speaks: With no further adieu, come up to the Star Table, "One Hit Wonder!"

[The audience and all the contestants clap as "One-Hit-Wonder" briskly walks up to receive his $2,500 check.]

[On-Hit-Wonder is a slender African-American male wearing a red Green Bay Packers fitted hat.]

[Host speaks to One-Hit-Wonder]
Host speaks: Yesterday you were feeling pretty confident…
One-Hit-Wonder speaks: You know the Vibe.

Host speaks: Okay?
Host speaks: Can I ask how you got your name?
One-Hit-Wonder Speaks: Your Honor…. You really don't want to know. I plead the 5th. We don't speak.

But you can buy my music at one hit wonder dot one. That's onehitwonder.one
And, if your an artist looking for somewhere to sell your music, holler at me.

Host speaks: Well, if you like his song folks, you know where to buy it.

[Host hands One-Hit-Wonder his microphone]
Host speaks: DJ, you know what to do!

[One-Hit-Wonder hears the music as it begins to play and stuffs his check into his back pocket.]
[An 808-heavy instrumental begins to play, and after a few seconds, One-Hit-Wonder begins to perform his song.]

One-Hit-Wonder speaks:

You rolled with me
When we went from state to state…
You never argued
There was no debate…
You're the only girl
I want in my face…
These other girls,
they cannot relate…
Mary
You were always there
when I needed you…
You believe in me
And I believe in you…
I got you…
And you got me…
Lets stack this money up…
And count this broccoli…

One-Hit-Wonder raps:
Do you remember when I met ya?
Those were the times…
You still give me inspiration…
For these poetic lines…
I met you cause my niggas…
Introduced me
to ya…
Felt as if
All my life
I already
knew ya…
And on our first date…
I tried to hit you
in the back of my car…
You were gone so quick
But you didn't leave me this far…
In this relationship…
And I soon hit it…
and quit it...
Yeah we broke up…
But of course
I had to get back with it…
I love you so much…
I know sometimes it looks bad…
Because I hit you…
and you choke me…
Whenever I'm mad...

But I like it when you're heated…
It compliments
your red hair...
And I can tell you…
that I cheated…
And you don't care…
So don't be scared…
Mary
Cause your cherry
Is the only cherry
I'll ever put
my mouth close to…
How could I doubt you?
Why would I ever go without you?
Don't you know?
Nothing's possible…
Without you?

You rolled with me
When we went from state to state…
We never argued
There was no debate…
You're the only girl
I want in my face…
These other girls,
they cannot relate…
Mary…
You were always there
when I needed you…
You believe in me
And I believe in you…
I got you…
And you got me…
Lets stack this money up
And count this broccoli…

One-Hit-Wonder speaks:
Mary…
would you marry me?
If my spirits were down…
Would you carry me?
Cause I would carry you…
across the threshold…
Me and you
together…
Until we get old…
And when I get home…
Just wanna brighten your day…
Give you a kiss
Then I'm piping away…
cause I'm the head of this household…
And you…
You're the Chief's wife…
So Mary Jane…
Just make sure
that I Chief right…
You make me sleep right…
You keep me so calm…
You're so fine…
I wish that I could grow a whole field of y'all…
You're the green apple
of my eye…
I picked you
straight from the tree…
That's how you got me so high…
So no matter what…
you're always a dime…
I might let the homies judge you…
but…
You'll always be mine…   (cont.)

And…
You'll always be fine…
You're the reason that
I'm on…
On the grind…
From nine to nine…
I thought marriage…
Would turn you
into a ball and chain…
But instead…
You bought me
all these chains…
So…
You're the only girl
I cannot replace…
And…
Even if you gain a lot of weight…
I'll be a fat kid…
and you know how to bake…
So I'ma love you more
every single day…

[THE CROWD GOES CRAZY]

One-Hit-Wonder raps:
You rolled with me
When we went from
state to state…
We never argued
There was no debate…
You're the only girl
I want in my face…
These other girls
they cannot relate…
Mary…
You were always there
when I needed you…
Mary…
You believe in me
And I believe in you…
I got you…
And you got me…
Lets stack this money up
And count this broccoli…

[One-Hit-Wonder hypes up the crowd]

One-Hit-Wonder speaks:
Now everybody say, "four-hundred-twenty nanos of
visible light, think about me and you, living the life."

One-Hit-Wonder repeats:
"four-hundred-twenty nanos of visible light, think
about me and you living the life."

[The performance comes to an end]

Host speaks: I think I might have just caught a
contact from that song. Wow…

Host speaks: and with that, the plot thickens because
we only have three more contestants left. So who
will they be?

[suspenseful music plays, at a low volume]

Host speaks:
Our next contestant, despite all the odds, has found
his way to this stage today, and is here to tell his story.
He pulled on our heartstrings yesterday— but—
will he be able to recreate the magic today, while
accompanied by music?

He came to the United States as a child, and has lived
all throughout the tri-state area, but now calls The
Bronx his home. With no further adieu, make your
way up to the stage, "The Nigerian Dream!"

[The audience and the other contestants clap as "The
Nigerian Dream" makes his way up to the stage to
receive his $2,500 check.]

[The Nigerian Dream has the remnant of a thick
African Accent]
Host speaks: So, how did you get your name?

[The Nigerian Dream pauses to reflect]
The Nigerian Dream speaks: Right now, in my
country, the dream. . . is to leave Nigeria.

That is how bad it is.

To go abroad, to London, to the United States, to Asia,
to anywhere. That is most people's dream.

I have seen relatives die from poverty and violence,
and I am not complaining, I am simply answering
your question.

"The Nigerian Dream" means— that a hero will leave
Nigeria… and come back to save Nigeria. That is "The
Nigerian Dream."

Host speaks: Okay, well. . . best of luck to your
endeavors, the world wants to hear your record.

[Host hands The Nigerian Dream his microphone]
Host speaks: DJ, let the dream begin.

[A wonderfully melodic afrobeat-style song begins
to play, and then the The Nigerian Dream begins to
perform]

The Nigerian Dream sings:
She get around cause she get around…
She get around cause she get around…
She get around cause she…
She get around cause she get around…
She get around cause she get around…
She get around cause she…

The Nigerian Dream sings:
She…
made it all the way…
To the west side of town…
She didn't have a car…
So I don't even know…
how…
I think she's getting getting getting getting…
Down…
Down down down…
Down down down…
Down down…
****
She get around cause she get around…
She get around cause she get around…
She get around cause she…
If you could see…
How she move around
By hitting half the town
Then nna proof would be…
But I don't blame her…
Oh no, she never knew…
Nobody taught her…
Think we
Maybe
blessed are you…

She get around cause she get around…
She get around cause she get around…
She get around cause she…
She get around cause she get around…
She get around cause she get around…
She get around cause she…

She...

She...
made it all the way
back to the South Side of town...
She was Southside bound
Cause the
south side
got
Down...
Nobody saw a thing
Her moving
No one heard a...
sound...
The bass
Thee trunk
Thee...
Pound Pound...
Pound Pound...
She get around
cause she get around...
She get around cause she get around...
She get around cause she...
She...
She better watch out
before
she has HIV...
Now she's in the hospital
With an
H. - I.V....
A baby on the way...
Oh no...
I hear crying...

She get around cause she get around…
She get around cause she get around…
She get around cause she…
She get around cause she get around…
She get around cause she get around…
She get around cause she…

The Nigerian Dream raps:

Yeah,
she mighta hopped up in your car once…
Yeah you mighta felt like a star once…
But now she's just a memory…
She died April first…
It feels like a century…
They say my cousin fucked with her…
That's why he's dead…
He gave it to his wife
And both of his two little kids…
And I'm like man…
I'ma never get to meet my cousins…
I'm like…
damn…
I feel like
Ain't nobody doing nothing…
Yeah…
That's why I teach and practice safe sex…
Yes Yes…
Condoms and latex…
Yes Yes…
Condoms and latex…

[A woman in the front row sheds a tear.]
[The African sounding melodic beat is powerful, along
with the spoken words of the performer.]

[The Camera changes introducing the next performer]

[Suspenseful Music Begins To Play]

Host speaks: Powerful powerful song.

Host speaks: Our next contestant, is performing a
brand new song. Yesterday he performed a song that
he wrote during a visit to Hollywood.

Host speaks:
I couldn't stop laughing yesterday,
when he said…
Maybe walk down the walk of fame…
Tomorrow
she's gon' have to take
The walk of shame…
I'm just looking for a Hollywood Ho…
I'm just looking for a Hollywood…
Hollywood Ho…

Hoe…

Host speaks:
Today he is pulling something else out of his sleeve
because he has chosen to perform an entirely different
song, titled, "SCRUB THE FLOOR." He stated he
originally made this song to make short-form videos
for a dancing app.

With no further adieu, come up to the stage, "Rizz
Kid"

[The audience cheers and claps as the contestant comes to the stage and accepts his $2,500 check.]

[Host speaks to Rizz Kid]
Host speaks: So Rizz Kid, how did you get that snazzy name of yours?
[Rizz Kid speaks with a Caribbean accent]
Rizz Kid speaks: My older brother dem gave me the name when I started making music my songs were always for the ladies.

Host speaks: Well hopefully none of those ladies distract you today because right now, you have $100,000 on the line. Are you ready?

Rizz Kid speaks: Always.

[Host hands Rizz Kid the microphone]
Host speaks: DJ, you know what to do!

[Music intro begins to play]
[the beat is lively, as we see the smiles and excitement on the faces of the audience.]

[Rizz Kid hears the music and begins to perform his song.]

Rizz Kid talks/sings:

Scrub the Floor Girl…
Come Work For Me…
If You're Hard working…
Let me see that you can do it…

Scrub the Floor Girl…
Pop that for me…
Twerk that for me…
Let me see that you can do it…

Rizz Kid raps:
Look… I'ma have em…
cooking n cleaning…
I'ma have em doing
things you don't believe in…
I'ma have em
going to work…
and going to church…
And you know it hurts…
I know it hurts when…
Your girl…
that didn't used to cook…
Now she knows
all the gourmet
cookbooks…
And your girl…
that didn't used to clean a thing…
Now I swear
that she's the Caribbean Dream…
Serving a Caribbean King…
Every night
before I sleep…
The royal penis gets cleaned…
So If ya… know what I mean
Then do the fuck what I say…
So…
If you know the dance
Scrub the floor
All day…
Like
Scrub the Floor Girl…
Come Work For Me…
If You're Hard working…
Let me see that you can do it…

Rizz Kid sings:

Scrub the Floor Girl…
Come Work For Me…
If You're Hard working…
Let me see that you can do it…

Scrub the Floor Girl…
Pop that for me…
Twerk that for me…
Let me see that you can do it…

Just pretend
You're at the gym
Girl
Doing your pilates…
Don't be lazy
Girl
Cause we just getting started…
On your hands
and knees
Girl
Don't hold back
No half hearted…
If you ain't
shed a tear
Then
you ain't really
Got it…
Ooh…
Sweat is glistening off her body…
Ooh…
Bright Crystal
Versace…
The way she cleans that wood…
Good wife
She embodies…
Presents in December
Even though
She's naughty…
you wish your kids
Called her mommy…
(cont.)

Wax onny
Wax offy…
I'm sensei
Splinter
Mister
Miagi…
Said lets kick it
in the future
Chop it up
Like karate…
Maybe we
can even have
A body party…
Ya dig…

[SUSPENSEFUL MUSIC PLAYS]
[Scene changes within the scene]

Host speaks: Wow. That was quite the performance.
I may have to let my fiancé have a listen to that song.

Host speaks: Well, we only have one contestant left.
But first off folks, lets take this moment, for a special
message from one of our sponsors (commercial)

[Commercial Comes on.]
Commercial speaks: Regardless of your budget, if you
want to learn how to mix and master music entirely
on your laptop, this book is definitely for you.
Mixing Mastering In The Box dot Com tells you
which plugins to buy, so that you can spend your
money wisely.
Learn the biggest secret, that large studios and mixing
and mastering houses don't want you to know. Go to
Mixing Mastering In The Box dot Com

[Scene changes within the scene]

[Suspenseful music plays]
[The Camera refocuses on the host]

Host speaks: We are back folks.
Our final contestant, will be receiving $2,500 dollars
in just a few moments, and then… will shoot his or
her shot at $100,000 dollars. Oh the suspense...

Remember… if your name is not called, this is not
a loss. The stars may not have aligned for you today,
but that does not mean that you are not a star.…. The
stars may align for you another day... if you continue
honing your craft and never give up.

Host speaks: Our final contestant, stated in his bio that the day he moved to Dallas is still the largest snowfall in the city of Dallas to this date. He stated that one of his best friends nicknamed him "Cold Boy" many years before that day, so that snowfall, was not just a coincidence— instead— it was the universe trying to tell us something.

Well, with no further adieu, Please… come on up to the stage…. "Veri Unfair!!"

[Veratis stands up and excitedly comes up to the stage to receive his $2,500.]

[The scene ends]

[Scene 23]
Title: Veratis and Nicholas at NYC Club
Location: New York Club
Length: 5 minutes

[We see Veratis and Nicholas at the bar.]
[Viewer is unsure of who has won the competition.]
[mood is lively, music is playing, inside of NYC nightclub.]

[Veratis speaks to the drink server]
Veratis speaks: hey, can I get two shots of your purest blue agave tequila?

Veratis speaks: and… can I get a bottle of water?

[The drink server pours two shots of blue agave tequila, and gives Veratis a bottled water, and then takes the one hundred dollar bill that Veratis has left on the counter.]

[Veratis opens the bottled water, drinks a small amount, and then pours his shot into the remaining water.]

Nicholas speaks: You mix water and tequila?

Veratis speaks: Yeah, I call it Patron-water. It tastes like sugar-water to me.

[Veratis holds up his bottle of water to make a toast]

Veratis speaks: To my friend Nicholas, whose beat making skills helped me to come out here. Though we didn't win, this is not the end.

Nicholas speaks: I can cheers to that
[Nicholas holds up his shot glass, and the two of them take a drink.]

[Nicholas uses his body language to point out a
specific girl in the nightclub]
Nicholas speaks: I think what's her name from the
competition is feeling you.
[Nicholas uses his body language to point out the girl]

[We see that Nicholas is pointing to "Mary Rich," the
beautiful hispanic girl from the competition.]

[Mary Rich and her group of girls see Veratis look
their way, and within a few moments, they walk
past Veratis, giving him an opportunity to introduce
himself]

[As Mary Rich walks past, Veratis, wanting to
introduce himself to *a fellow contestant*, stops her, to
introduce himself.]
[Veratis reaches out his hand to *gently* touch the arm
of Mary Rich]
Veratis speaks: Hey

Mary Rich speaks: Hey.
Veratis speaks: I liked your song.
Mary Rich speaks: (looking up at Veratis with awe)
Thank you.
Mary Rich speaks: Texas Boy.
Veratis speaks: Wait. Where are you from?

Mary Rich speaks: I'm from Arlington.
Veratis speaks: Oh, wow, so what do you do in
Arlington?

Arlington is a large city 20 miles west of downtown Dallas.

Veratis speaks: Are you going to school or anything?

Mary Rich speaks: No, no school…

Mary Rich speaks: You promise not to judge me?
[Veratis holds his right hand up as if he is taking an oath]
Veratis speaks: I promise. I won't judge.

Mary Rich speaks: I'm a dancer.
Veratis speaks: Okay, like where?

Mary Rich speaks: Cabaret most of the time, sometimes Bucks, or Dolls.

Mary Rich speaks: Are you guys staying at the hotel where everyone is staying?
Veratis speaks: Yeah, we are.
Mary Rich speaks: I'm in room 104.

Veratis speaks: I heard all the rooms on the first floor have hot tubs?
Mary Rich speaks: My room has a one.
Mary Rich speaks: I've just been so lonely out here though.
Mary Rich speaks: Are you going to buy me a drink? (She asks sweetly and nicely)

Veratis speaks: I got you.
Veratis speaks: Shots on me. Your girls want anything?

[The scene ends]

[Scene 24]
Title: Nicholas talks to friend of Mary Rich
Location: New York Club
Length: 2 minutes

[Fast Pace EDM/House/Electronic Music Plays]
[As the camera pans from one side of the night club
to the other, we see the club is dark and filled with
people dancing, go-go dancers on elevated platforms,
and party people.]

[As the camera pans, the image becomes
hazy and unclear.][We see an unknown young man
with his back against the wall, while an unknown girl
grinds up against him.][but the image is too blurry for
us to discern who the individuals are.]

[As we watch the boy and girl dance, the tempo of the
music slows down, and the picture becomes grainier
and even more unclear.]

[Scene changes within the scene]
[The speed of the music returns to regular speed, and we see Nicholas and Lena, the friend of Mary Rich, at a table.]

[Lena speaks loudly in order for Nicholas to hear her over the music]
Lena speaks: So, you are a producer?
Nicholas speaks: Yeah
Lena speaks: Did you make any of the songs from the competition?
Nicholas speaks: Yeah, I made Veratis's beat for "One Day I'ma Be A Star."
Lena speaks: I love music; I used to sing in my school's choir, and I play violin.
Nicholas speaks: Wow, maybe we can work together, on a beat.
Lena speaks: That would be awesome.
Nicholas speaks: You wanna get out of here? this really isn't my scene.
Lena speaks: Sure, why not.
Nicholas speaks: What about your girl? Maybe we should bring her and Veratis?
Lena speaks: She'll be fine. She's a big girl.
Lena speaks: And I think she likes your friend.

[For a brief moment the camera focuses on Mary Rich and Veratis, who are standing at another end of the nightclub.]
[We see Mary Rich touch Veratis's hand.]
Nicholas speaks: Yeah, let's get out of here.
[Nicholas and Lena begin to grab their jackets.]

[Scene 25]
Title: The Morning After
Location: New York Hotel
Length: 5 minutes

[Visual cues show that the time of the day is morning.]
[We see the outside of the New York Hotel.]

[Veratis walks back into his hotel room, after he has
been out all night.]

[Veratis sees Nicholas, and shakes him, to wake him up]
Veratis speaks: Nicholas, wake up.

[To Veratis's surprise, there is a girl under the blanket.
She gets up, immediately surprised, and gets her
things and rushes out the door.]
Veratis speaks: Hey wait. Where's Nick?

[Veratis smiles, congratulating Nick in his mind]

[Moments later, Nicholas walks through the door with
food from the hotel's free breakfast.]
Veratis speaks: Your girl just left. Where you been?
Nicholas speaks: I had to get free breakfast. It's free.

Veratis speaks: Did you hit that?
Nicholas speaks: The way she cleaned my wood.
Good wife she embody.

[Veratis laughs]

Nicholas speaks: What about you?... your gold digger?

Vertis speaks: Why is she a gold digger?
Nicholas speaks: Bro, her name is *Marry* Rich.

[Veratis, realizing the play on words, laughs]

Veratis speaks: Her name is Maria Ricardo.
Nicholas speaks: Oh. Okay.

Nicholas speaks: But did you smash?

[Veratis haughtily laughs.]
Veratis speaks: A Player does not kiss and tell my friend.

Nicholas speaks: Well, all of this might not be new to you Veratis… but for me, I could get used to being a superstar producer.

Nicholas speaks: She was all over me V. She wants me to produce beats for her because she sings.

Nicholas speaks: I've been hanging out in the wrong circle.

Veratis speaks: Well. It's about to get even better.
[Veratis pulls out $1,200 dollars from his pocket.]
Veratis speaks: This is yours.

Nicholas speaks: Naw, that is yours Veratis.

Veratis speaks: You made the beat. This is yours.
[Veratis hands Nicholas the money.]

[Nicholas is reluctant to accept the money, but eventually accepts the gift]
Nicholas speaks: Thanks man. I appreciate it.
Veratis speaks: Naw… Thank you.

Nicholas speaks: Hey V, the girl who just left, (Lena)
last night, she asked if we ever throw parties.

Nicholas speaks: I was just thinking, you won this
money, and even though you didn't win the big prize,
back at school, you got motion right now. Why don't
we flip this money?
Nicholas speaks: Why don't we shoot a video?
[Veratis wears a questioning look on his face]
Veratis speaks: How are we gonna flip the money and
spend money to shoot a video?

Nicholas speaks: Not if we throw a party, and we
charge everyone to get into the party, and that's where
we shoot the video.

Nicholas speaks: Strobush has a camera...
and I got a [insert camera name here][SPONSOR
OPPORTUNITY]

Veratis speaks: You wanna throw a party?
Nicholas speaks: Yeah… that's money for studio time
and profit.
Veratis speaks: Sounds good, but where?
Nicholas speaks: You realize where I live right?
Nicholas speaks: We just rent out "The Palace" on the
top floor. It holds 500 people.
Nicholas speaks: And get the word out to all the dorms.
[Veratis pauses for a moment.]
[He contemplates the possibilities.]
[Then he speaks.]
Veratis speaks: Let's pack that bitch.

[The scene ends]

[Scene 26]
Title: Veratis calls Bartender
Location: New York Hotel
Length: 1 minute

[We see Veratis packing his clothes.]
[Veratis stops packing his clothing.]
[Veratis dials his phone.]

[We hear a phone's ringing tone]

[Bartender answers phone]
Bartender speaks via phone: Hey Rap Star.
Veratis speaks via phone: Hey Babe. How are you?
Bartender speaks via phone: I texted you last night
Bartender speaks: You didn't answer.
Veratis speaks: Yeah babe, I was just so tired after
these last few days. I knocked out…
Veratis speaks via phone: But is everything okay?
Bartender speaks via phone: Yeah I'm good, I'm just
missing you.
Veratis speaks: I miss you too babe.
Veratis speaks: I'll be back tomorrow. Can you pick
me up from the airport?
Bartender speaks: Of course… Just tell me when.
[The scene ends]

[Scene 27]
Title: View of the Star-lit Sky
Location: The Sky
Length: 1 minute

[We see a view of the night sky, lit up with stars.]
[We see flying objects.]
[The peaceful night sky adds a euphoric calming element to the scene transition]

[Scene 28]
Title: Dallas Love
Location: Dallas Love Field Airport
Length: 1 minute

[Visual cues show that the time of day is morning.]
[We hear the sound of traffic, cars, and horns.]
[We see Bartender waiting inside of her vehicle,
outside of the airport.]

[We wait for a few moments.]

[We now see Veratis as he exits the airport.]

[Veratis scans the cars.]
[Veratis scans the cars, and eventually recognizes
Bartender in her car.]

[Veratis approaches the vehicle and enters the car.]
Veratis speaks: Hey babe.

[The scene ends]

[Scene 29]
Title: The Sex Scene
Location: Bartender's Apartment
Length: 5 minute

[Bartender's front door opens.]
[Bartender and Veratis cannot let go of each other,
and they almost fall over as they enter into the
apartment.]
[As they stumble across the room, they passionately
kiss.][The couple continues kissing as they make their
way to Bartender's standing desk.]
[Bartender begins to rub Veratis's zipper area,
and Veratis begins to remove Bartender's blouse as he
sucks her neck.]
[The spaghetti strap of Bartender's bra falls onto the
side of her arm as he removes her bra.]

[Bartender removes Veratis's belt as Veratis unzips
the back of her skirt, and Bartender's skirt falls to the
ground.]
[Bartender lays her back on the desk.]
[Her french braids hang over the far side of the desk.]
[As Veratis continues to kiss her, Veratis softly
squeezes her breasts, and in the same motion pulls
down her bra, exposing her breasts.
Veratis squeezes her breasts
and begins to suck her succulent bust.]
[The scene ends]

[Scene 30]
Title: Pre-Video Shoot
Location: The Palace (top floor of Nick's Apartment)
Length: 5 minute

[Strobush holds a video camera as he records Nicholas and Veratis.]

[The group of boys walk through "The Palace," the venue where they will be holding the party.]

Nicholas speaks: Today we secured the Venue, Seventeen-Fifty cash. Normally, you have to pay women to be in your videos.

But, due to supply and demand, that we learned in our economics classes, ladies you get the opportunity to be in a major music video, for only $20 dollars.

And fellas, $50, gets you the chance to be remembered... because this is a moment.

Veratis speaks: I know my Alphas will be out here. Anybody who is anybody will be out here. Yes sir. So mark your calendars and come dressed to impress.

Come and shine with me forever.

[The scene ends]

[Scene 31]
Title: The Rise to the Occasion
Location: Multiple Locations
Length: 30 seconds

1 - Scene - Bartender calls up friend at the dorms and tells her about the party.

2 - Scene - Girl at the dorms posts the party info onto a popular social website.

3 - Scene - A group of female roommates crowd around a computer, reading the party's invite information.

4 - Scene - The captain of the football team calls up his teammates and lets them know, Veratis's party is going to be "the party of the year."

5 - Scene - A sorority girls takes a call from her football player boyfriend.

6 - Scene - A group of boys talk excitedly amongst themselves about how all the sororities will be at the party.

7 - Scene - Lena, friend of Mary Rich, calls Mary Rich, in order to tell her about party, and Mary Rich states *that she has been throwing up all day.*

[Scene 32]
Title: DAY OF THE OCCASION
Location: The Plex, Nicholas's Building
Length: 1 minutes

[The time of day is late afternoon. We see a beer truck stop directly in front of The Plex, and two delivery men begin to bring multiple kegs of beer inside.]

[Scene changes within the scene]
[We see upstairs -"The Palace"- top floor of The Plex.]

[The delivery men enter, and Veratis tells them where to set the kegs.]
Veratis speaks: Hey you guys can put the kegs over here.

[Nicholas enters]
Nicholas speaks: We got bottles on top of bottles. We got top shelf vodka. We got blue agave tequila. We got brown, we got white. Everything we ordered is here.

[Veratis speaks to Nick]
Veratis speaks: This is about to be lit.

[The scene ends]

[Scene 33]
Title: "One Day I'ma Be A Star" Video Shoot
Location: The Palace, Top Floor
Length: 5 minutes

[THE PARTY HAS BEGUN]
[amazing music is playing]

[Veratis is wearing a dark sweatshirt that says "Security" in yellow letters, and is holding a capacity counter.]

[people are entering the party while Nicholas and Veratis work the door.]

[Veratis speaks loudly over the music]
Veratis speaks: We gotta have at least 100 people here already.

[As Veratis finishes his sentence, a very beautiful girl enters the scene, with a pack of beautiful girls behind her.]

Veratis speaks: Hello ladies; do you have your e-tickets?

[Cyn (the very beautiful girl) hands Veratis her phone, and Veratis hands it back to her motioning for her and the group of girls to enter.]

Veratis speaks: Ladies the cameras are rolling all night, so have a good time.
[The women enter.]

Nicholas speaks: How do you do it V?
Veratis speaks: How do I do what?
Nicholas speaks: How do you play it so cool around
women?

Nicholas speaks: She said she was gonna come.
Nicholas speaks: I think I texted her too many times.

Veratis speaks: Who?

Nicholas speaks: Lena.

Veratis speaks: Who is Lena?

Nicholas speaks: Your side chick from New York's
friend.

Veratis speaks: She's not my side chick.

Nicholas speaks: Okay. Whatever you say. But how do
you do it? *how do you have the courage to talk to any
woman?*

[Veratis speaks loudly because of the music playing]
Veratis speaks: You have to put your fear to the side…

It's okay to be scared, but you can't let your fear
control you.
Veratis speaks: Just ask her if she wants a drink
or ask her name.

Ask her how her night is going. Compliment her.
Find out where she is from.

[The DJ begins to speak]
DJ speaks: The cameras are rolling. The drinks are flowing. If you want to be in the video, whenever this song plays right here, it's a good idea to be in front of a camera.
["One day I'ma be a Star," the song, begins to play.]

[Scene changes within the scene]
[In the women's restroom, we see a group of girls having a conversation.]
Paris speaks: He is so cute. I'm going to suck his dick tonight.
Cyn speaks: You're such a little hoe.
Paris speaks: Yeah, I am!

[The camera cuts back to the main party]

[As the song plays, lights shine on Veratis as he says the words to his song.]
Veratis wears a shirt that says "Security," but ironically, the two men on his side look like bodyguards.

Veratis speaks:
I'ma Be…
I'ma Be…
I'ma Be…
I'ma Be…
I'ma Be…
I'ma Be A Star…
I'ma Be A Star…

Stars…
Cowboys…
Texas Rangers…
Big titty chicks…
That say hello to strangers…
But I got a cd,
So she thinks she knows me…
Hydrogen…
Helium…
Told the bitch to blow me…

[The camera cuts to a different location.]
[Location: Bartender's Bar]

[Bartender is at work, finishing up her shift for the night.]
Bartender's coworker speaks: Any plans for tonight? Are you going to that big party at The Plex?

Bartender speaks: Coincidentally I am… That's my boyfriend's party.

[Scene changes within the scene]

[The camera cuts back to the main party]
[Veratis continues rapping his lyrics on camera.]
[Veratis raps]

I pull hoes…
Call it gravitation…
You pull nothing…
Call it masturbation…
With these hoes, no procrastination…
Shit I hit the first night…
Then it's back to chasin…
The shit that makes the world go round…
Yeahhhhh…
The shit that makes your girl go down…
Yeeahhhh…

[Time advances forward.]
[We hear Veratis's song finishing, and a new song is beginning to play.]

[Paris and Cyn, the girls from the restroom, and a group of girls all dressed as cheerleaders, come up to Veratis.]

[The girls are all dressed in blue and white Cowboy replica cheerleader uniforms, with stars and fringe on the vests.]

[Paris looks up at Veratis to speak to him.]
Paris speaks: How do we look? (Referring to the cheerleader uniforms) We wanted to make sure you put us in your video.

Veratis speaks: Y'all are doing your thing. I'll tell my camera man to make sure he gets you when the song plays.

[Paris leans in and whispers in Veratis's ear]
Paris speaks: And I wanna make a video with just you later tonight.

[Veratis chuckles]
Veratis speaks: I'm not sure what type of video you mean. I guess I am flattered, but I will have to decline. Thank you though.

[Veratis motions to Strobush and the camera crew to get footage of the girls in their cheerleader uniforms.]

Veratis speaks: Hey, make sure you get lots of footage. And make sure to get them when the song plays again.

[Veratis touches the arm of Paris as he bids her farewell.]
Veratis speaks: Take care of yourself.

[Veratis looks at his phone.]
[Veratis sees Bartender is calling him and attempts to move to a quieter place to answer the call.]

[Veratis answers the call.]
Veratis speaks: Hey babe.
Bartender speaks: Hey, I'm still closing down. I'm running a little late, but I want to make it there babe.
Veratis speaks: Okay, don't worry. I'll see you when you get here.
Bartender speaks: Okay, I'll see you. Miss you.

[Veratis and Bartender end their call, and Veratis looks at his phone.]
[Veratis realizes that he has 5 missed text messages.]

[Veratis looks to see who the messages are from.]
[Veratis sees the messages are all from Mary Rich.]

Text Messages Read:
"Hey"
"I need to talk to you"

"I have something important I have to tell you"
"Can you please call me"

[Veratis reconfirms that all the messages are from
Mary Rich]

"Hey"
"I need to talk to you"
"Please, do not do this to me."
"Can you please call me"

[Veratis stops and replies to Mary Rich.]
Veratis's Text reads: "Maria, you can't just text me
anyhow. I have a girlfriend."

[Maria responds back,]
Text: "I'm pregnant"

(TO BE CONTINUED. . . .)

END OF PART ONE

[Scene 34] [Sneak Peek]
Title: The Morning After Video Shoot
Location: Bartender's Apartment

[We see the sun rising, and we hear the sounds of a Dallas morning.]
[Visual cues show us that the time of the day is morning]
[Camera cuts to inside of the apartment.]
[We see Veratis laying in bed]

[Bartender wakes up next to Veratis. . . and snuggles up next to him]
Bartender speaks: Veratis, do you love me?

Acknowledgement

I want to thank each and every one of you who purchased this book. I hope you all enjoyed reading the first part of Beloved of the Stars.

Your support will help bring to life the upcoming projects listed below & more from MMITB Publishing.

Good things are coming your way.

UPCOMING PROJECTS FROM MMITB PUBLISHING

Beloved of the Stars - Part 2
The second and final chapter of Beloved of the Stars.

M.R.S. Degree (the mp3 & the book)
The story of Kennedy Evermore, an African American pre-med student, in Atlanta, who simply wanted to get married before her first year of med school.

Gosh Darnit Dallas
The story of Dallas, a young man who just happens to have the biggest jerk of a boss.

www.ingramcontent.com/pod-product-compliance
Lightning Source LLC
Chambersburg PA
CBHW030651110726
47901CB00002B/664